This edition published by Parragon Books Ltd in 2014

Parragon Books Ltd
Chartist House
15–17 Trim Street
Bath BA1 1HA, UK
www.parragon.com

ISBN 978-1-4723-7240-6

Printed in China

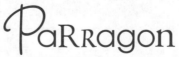

Bath · New York · Cologne · Melbourne · Delhi
Hong Kong · Shenzhen · Singapore · Amsterdam

Minnie is hard at work in her busy Bow-tique.
"Oh, Cuckoo-Loca," says Minnie, "isn't my new
magic bejeweller fantastic?"

Suddenly, Minnie hears giggling!
"Who's making that noise?" she says.
"It's us, Aunt Minnie!" shout Millie and Melody,
jumping out at her.

Delighted, Minnie greets her twin nieces. "Hello, Millie! Hello, Melody!"

The girls begin to run around the Bow-tique.

Oh, no! They accidentally knock over boxes of bows and beads!

"Can we help you make stuff today?" Millie asks.
"We promise to be extra good," adds Melody.

Cuckoo-Loca looks at the mess the girls have already made. "Famous last words," she says.

"I was just thinking how nice it would be to have two helpers today," says Minnie. "Why don't you unpack that box of ribbons for me?"

"Yay!" shout Millie and Melody.

Just then, Daisy Duck rushes into the shop.

"Minnie!" she calls excitedly. "You're never going to believe it…. "

Oops-a-daisy! She slips on the spilled beads and falls!

"Oh, Daisy!" cries Minnie. "Are you alright?"

"Never better," says Daisy. "Guess what famous movie superstar is on her way over to the Bow-tique right now?"

"Penelope Poodle?" guesses Minnie.

"Right!" cries Daisy. "I've just got off the phone with her people. They made me promise that Penelope could shop in total peace and quiet."

Suddenly, Millie and Melody
zoom past Daisy, nearly
knocking her over.

"Hi, Daisy," the twins
shout. "Sorry about the beads!

Daisy looks at the girls and
sighs. "Minnie, the twins are
not total peace and quiet."

Minnie giggles. "Normally, that's true.
But they've promised to be extra good today."
Millie and Melody reach for some spools of
colourful ribbon.

Uh-oh! Looks like the helpers
need some help!
"Oops! Sorry, Aunt Minnie!"

Just then, there's a huge commotion outside.

Penelope Poodle has arrived!

Excited fans and photographers crowd around the famous movie star. "Look this way, Miss Poodle," shouts a photographer. "Can we get a smile?"

"Oh!" cries Daisy. "She's here!"

Daisy hurries to clean up the mess.

The glamorous Penelope Poodle glides
through the door.

"Welcome to my Bow-tique," says Minnie.

"Hello," says Penelope. "You must help me. I'm
accepting a Golden Bone award in less than an hour,
and I need something fabulous to wear!"

Suddenly, Millie and Melody race past Penelope!
"Beep, beep!" shouts Millie.
"Coming through!" warns Melody.

Penelope Poodle gasps.
that I could shop in total
Cuckoo-Loca pops up t
"Love your movies. Even t
May I have your autograp

," Daisy says firmly. "Minnie was
oodle that one-of-a-kind thing she

p. "One-of-a-kind?"

Thinking fast,
made with her
"I call it th
Penelope

nd Melody crash into some

lays!

he twins.

They knock over racks of bows, ribbons and even a can of paint.

The paint splatters everywhere!

Penelope Poodle has had enough. "I can see that coming here was a mistake."

"I am positive I can find you something gorgeous to wear," Minnie says, "if you'll just wait."

"Wait?" says Penelope. "I can't waste another moment! I simply must go! What have those little monsters done to me?"

"Oh, they're not little monsters," says Minnie. "They're little helpers!"

She quickly adds bows and jewels to the twins' handiwork. "I think they're on to something!"

Penelope Poodle looks in the mirror.
"I look fabulous!" she says. "You're brilliant!"
Minnie smiles sweetly.
"That's what I always say," Daisy agrees.

Everyone loves Penelope's new outfit.

"Miss Poodle!" calls a fan. "That's a fantastic look!"

"Who are you wearing?" asks a photographer.

Penelope smiles. "Who else? Minnie Mouse, of course!"

Millie and Melody look at the mess they have made in the Bow-tique.

"We'll clean up for you, Aunt Minnie," they promise.

Daisy lets out a sigh of relief. "I don't know how you do it," she says, shaking her head.

"Oh, Daisy," says Minnie, "I'm just trying to spread happiness, one bow at a time."